This story is for Jackson Hurwood.—CM

My dedication goes to Alexandra.—NC

Pirates Eat Porridge

CHRISTOPHER MORGAN
AND NEIL CURTIS

A NEAL PORTER BOOK
ROARING BROOK PRESS
NEW YORK

Text copyright © 2006 by Christopher Morgan
Illustrations copyright © 2006 by Neil Curtis
A Neal Porter Book
Published by Roaring Brook Press
Roaring Brook Press is a division of Holtzbrinck Publishing Holdings
Limited Partnership
175 Fifth Avenue, New York, New York 10010
www.roaringbrookpress.com

Distributed in Canada by H. B. Fenn and Company, Ltd.

Library of Congress Cataloging-in-Publication Data
Morgan, Christopher, 1956-
Pirates eat porridge / Christopher Morgan and [illustrated by] Neil Curtis.
— 1st American ed.
p. cm.
"A Neal Porter book."
Summary: While Mom and Dad are away, a pirate takes Billy and his sister
Heidi on a wild adventure, sailing their "fish-finger" house to Itchy Ear
Island and telling them quirky facts about pirates, parrots, and cabbages.
ISBN-13: 978-1-59643-304-5 ISBN-10: 1-59643-304-3
[1. Pirates—Fiction. 2. Brothers and sisters—Fiction. 3. Humorous stories.]
I. Curtis, Neil, ill. II. Title.
PZ7.M821137Pk 2007 [E]—dc22 2007002171

Roaring Brook Press books are available for special promotions
and premiums.
For details, contact: Director of Special Markets, Holtzbrinck Publishers.

Printed in the United States of America
First American edition September 2007
2 4 6 8 10 9 7 5 3 1

Billy loved being in his tree house.

Up here, he could see the mountains to the east, the sea to the south, the buildings of the city to the west, and all sorts of interesting things in the sky.

He liked to lean out of the window and ask himself questions:

Do clouds talk to each other?

Do flying fish have nests?

Who tells the tide to go out?

He was just wondering whether
jellyfish might taste like jelly when a
large sheet of paper blew in through the
window and rolled itself up like a scroll
at his feet.

It had

written on it in big, bold letters.

Suddenly, Billy's sister, Heidi, jumped over the top of the ladder and tumbled into the tree house.

"There's a pirate at our door!"

"A pirate?"

"A pirate. And a *pig*."

"I'd better go and see."

"What do you want?"

Billy's voice sounded small. He tried again.

"What do you want?"

"Not very polite are we, Mr. Fishcake? Talking like that to a gentleman who knocks on your door.

"It so happens that a treasure map blew over your back fence. I was chasing it up the street. I saw you pick it up. It's mine. It's nobody else's. I want it. And while I'm here . . .

"I want me
BREAKFAST."

And with that, the pirate pushed past Billy and stomped and rolled down the hallway, his big sea boot thumping on the floorboards.

He poked at the pictures on the walls as he went, until they all hung crooked. Then he stopped and smiled at his work.

Heidi stood in the kitchen doorway with her arms crossed.

"You can't have breakfast. It's almost dinnertime."

"Dinnertime, is it? Well I'll be a squid's bottom. I thought it was breakfast-time.

"Not to worry—I can have porridge for dinner."

He scratched his chin.

"Tell me, what sort of a ship is this anyway?"

"This isn't a ship. It's our house," said Heidi.

"A house, is it? Well shiver me timbers. I always wondered what one looked like on the inside.

"I wonder where the sails are? Where's the galley? Perhaps it's this way. C'mon, Polly."

And he thumped past Heidi into the kitchen.

The pirate sat in Dad's chair and waved his spoon in the air.

"BUMS DOWN, SAILORS. BUMS DOWN."

He looked at the empty space on the table in front of him, and then he looked at Heidi.

"I'm ready. Where's my porridge?"

Heidi gave Billy a look. Billy shrugged his shoulders and shook his head.

"Your porridge," Heidi said slowly, "is probably on your ship."

The pirate banged his spoon on the table.

"Mr. Fishcake, what's wrong with her? She doesn't speak to me very nicely. I take it she's your sister?"

Billy nodded.

"Don't worry. I have a way with sisters."

He banged his spoon on the table again, then he made a ferocious face.

"Hey, you! Miss Fishnose!

"WHERE'S MY PORRIDGE?

"WHERE'S MY PORRIDGE?

"WHERE'S MY PORRIDDDGGE?"

There was silence.

No one spoke to Heidi that way. No one. Her face began to turn *very* red.

"P-p-perhaps your pig knows where your porridge is?" asked Billy quickly.

The pirate leaped from his seat.

"He's not a pig. He's a parrot. How could you say such a thing?"

"Oh, I'm sorry," said Billy. "I thought he was a . . . It's just that he looks like a . . . "

"He *is* a pig!" said Heidi.

"Twoink. Twoink. Twoink?" said the pig.

"I know," said the pirate, looking down at the pig. "She is a little bit of a grump pot. Don't listen to her. You're a parrot, not a pig. There's a clever little bird."

"Twoink," said the pig contentedly, and leaped onto the pirate's shoulder.

"Now," said the pirate, "who is the captain of this here fish-finger house?"

"We have two captains. Mom and Dad. They're at the supermarket," said Heidi.

"What's a supermarket?" asked the pirate.

"It's where people buy food," said Billy.

"You mean you have to buy it? I don't believe you."

"Yes, we do have to buy it. How would *you* get it?" asked Heidi.

The pirate scratched his ear with the spoon.

"Well, Miss Fishnose, the street is full of these here fish-finger houses. All of them are standing still. I would just go into any one of them and take what I need. I'd never go hungry. Never."

"But they're our neighbors," said Heidi.

"And they've got a dog," added Billy, pointing to the house next door.

"Neighbors? When you're a pirate, the only neighbors you have are stingrays, seals, and sharks."

He thought for a second.

"And sometimes elephants. When they're out for a swim."

"I didn't know elephants could swim," said Billy.

"Oh, they can swim all right, Mr. Fishcake. It's pirates who can't swim."

"You can't swim?" asked Heidi.

"Oh, no," said the pirate. "Pirates prefer to walk along the bottom of the sea."

"But how do you breathe?"

"That's the problem, Miss Fishnose. We can't. That's why we have ships—so we can walk up and down on them with our heads held up high and our big hats on."

He leaned toward Heidi as if he were about to tell her a great secret.

"Ships go on *top* of the water."

He nodded his head wisely. Then he turned to Billy.

"Now I want my treasure map back, Mr. Fishnose. Give it to me."

Billy pulled the roll of paper from his sock and laid it across the table.

"That's not a treasure map," said Heidi. "It's just a picture of an island."

"It does say

across the top," said Billy quietly.

"Oh, it's a treasure map all right, Miss Fishnose," said the pirate. "This picture here is the first clue to where the treasure is hidden. . . . And wobble me noggin!! If it isn't Itchy Ear Island!"

"It is *not*," said Heidi. "It's Pelican Island. It's written right here."

"It's Itchy Ear Island, Miss Fishnose. That pelican business is just a pirate warning."

"A pirate warning?" asked Billy.

"A pirate warning," said the pirate. He shivered like a jellyfish. "To remind pirates everywhere to get home before dark."

"But why?" asked Heidi.

"*Why?*" whispered the pirate. His teeth began to chatter so loudly that Heidi and Billy had to cover their ears with their hands. "Because that is when the giant pelicans come out and spit in the eyes of pirates. Everybody knows that, too."

"You look a bit frightened," said Heidi.

"I am not," yelled the pirate.

"Is that why some pirates wear eye patches?" asked Billy.

The pirate tried to smile, but his lips were, for a moment, stuck together.

"That's exactly right, Mr. Fishcake. They're the ones who stayed out too late."

The pig let out a little squeal.

"Settle down, Polly. We'll be safe in bed before it gets dark."

He turned to the children. "Giant pelicans don't much like parrots, either," he explained. Then he shuddered and looked back at the picture.

"This is Itchy Ear Island, all right. I know it because that's where I do my washing. If you look closely at the palm tree on the left, you can see my clothesline."

"Do pirates wash their clothes?" asked Billy, disappointed.

"I doubt it," said Heidi, and stared pointedly at the pirate's shirt.

"Of course pirates wash their clothes. What a squiddly, bottomly question," said the pirate.

"Another reason I know this particular island so well is because once, by accident, I left a shipmate behind there.

"It took me a year to realize what had happened. A whole year. I didn't mind much, though. He had a bad, bad habit. He was a peanut spitter. The worst kind of spitter there can be.

"Berry Berry Barry Barton was his name. I sailed straight back to get him when I noticed he was gone.

When I came ashore, he was sitting in the sand spitting peanuts out of his mouth."

"Was he pleased to see you?" asked Billy.

"I think so. He didn't say anything. His mouth was full of peanuts. He spat them at me while I hung out my washing."

The pirate smiled sweetly.

"So I left him there again."

"Oh," said Billy.

"Oh," said Heidi.

"So . . . if it was a year before you went back to Itchy Ear Island, then you only wash your clothes once a year," said Billy, thinking aloud.

"That's right. How often do you wash yours? If I did it any more they would fall apart and I'd have to go to sea in my underpants."

He shivered at the thought, then jumped to his feet.

"Now, all hands on deck!"

"Excuse me?" said Heidi.

The pirate ignored her. He grabbed some sheets from the washing pile.

"Sails!"

Then he stuck Heidi's favorite purple shirt into his pocket.

"And a flag!"

He stood to attention and saluted. So did Billy. Heidi rolled her eyes.

"To the masts! Onto the roof! We'll sail this fish-finger house to Itchy Ear Island."

And with that, he was out the door.

"Hoist the sails! Man the poop deck! Roll out the cannons! Stack up the cabbages! Raise the flag! Let's go! There's no time to lose."

"Stack what cabbages?" asked Billy.

"The cannonball cabbages, of course. What do *you* use for cannonballs?"

Heidi cleared her throat. "Pirate, this is our house. It is not a ship. And there's no water. We won't be sailing anywhere."

"Miss Fishnose," sighed the pirate, "everything is a ship. Everything. And as for water, it's everywhere. Don't you know anything? This concrete and dirt is just sitting on top of the ocean, that's all. It will sink to the bottom as soon as the wind fills the sails."

And he was right. That is exactly what happened.

Soon, they were on the open sea. Spray hit their faces.

"Look!" Billy yelled to Heidi.

His tree house was floating along behind, rising and falling in the waves. It was attached to the house by the clothesline.

The pirate strode across the roof and stood by the chimney.

"Miss Fishnose, pass me the compass."

"We don't have a compass," said Heidi, a little distracted.

"Well I'll be a pair of prawn's pajamas! How do you tell which direction you are traveling in?"

"I can tell directions," said Billy.

"Can you now?" asked the pirate. "Which direction are we moving in, then?"

"South by southwest," said Billy without hesitation.

"Sheets and sheets of water!" boomed the pirate. "You *are* a good compass, Mr. Fishcake. We need to turn a little. Miss Fishnose, point me to the steering wheel."

"There isn't one." Heidi shrugged. "This is a house, not a ship."

"Then we'll have to lean. On the count of four. One . . . two . . . ah?"

"Twoink," said the pig.

"Three," whispered Billy.

"Three . . . **four** . . . **lean.**"

The house turned.

"So what do pirates do, anyway?" asked Billy after they'd been sailing for a while.

The pirate put one hand up to shade his eyes as he looked out over the horizon.

"Pirates look for buried treasure, Mr. Fishcake. Everybody knows that. And when we find it, we dive our hands into it and laugh very loudly.

"HA HA HA!"

"Why?" asked Heidi.

"What do you mean *why*?" said the pirate.

"Why do you dive your hands into it and laugh loudly?"

"I don't know. Because that's what I was taught to do."

"Where did you learn to do that?" asked Billy.

"At Pirate School. Where else would I learn to do it?"

"I think I'd like to go to Pirate School," announced Billy.

"Maybe I'd like to go to Pirate School, too," said Heidi.

"Oh, would you now? So you two
were born in a seagull's nest, were you?

Your brothers and sisters were all baby seagulls? Because that's what you need to become a pirate. They don't let just anybody into Pirate School, you know."

The pirate put his hands on his hips.

"And another thing. You have to be able to speak Seagullese."

"What's that?"

"The language that seagulls speak, of course. How else do you think they talk to each other?"

"I didn't know that they *could* talk to each other," Heidi admitted.

"So, how do you think they know where the rotten fish are? How do they know who is eating a sandwich?"

He looked out to sea.

"Top of my class, I was. Number one. Voted the child most likely to grow into the ugliest pirate. I ate more live worms and fried blowflies than anybody. And as for the Golden Crab Claw award—"

"What's that?" interrupted Billy.

"Well I'll be blown down a whale's sock. You don't know what the Golden Crab Claw award is?

"What sort of children are you? What sort of school do you go to? Don't those captains of yours tell you anything?"

"Our parents have never told us about that award," said Heidi. "We didn't even know there was a Pirate School."

"Unbelievable! What cruelty! Ah well, such is life . . . on the land. The Golden Crab Claw award is given each year by the bent-up, creaky old pirates who run the Land Ahoy Cabbage Shop on Belly Button Island."

"Cabbage shop?"

"That's right. Any type of cabbage you want. Any way you want it. Those old pirates know more about cabbages than anybody I have ever met before."

He leaned forward and whispered,

"Although most pirates know a fair bit about cabbages."

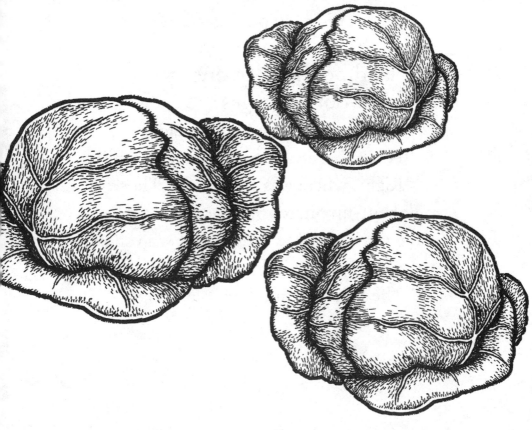

"Why?" asked Heidi.

"Why what?"

"Why do pirates know about cabbages?"

"Because it's a good vegetable.
Why should you people on
the land be the only ones to
know about cabbages?"

"There's no reason," said Heidi.

"None that I can think of," added Billy.

"Right, where was I? Oh, yes. Those
old, bent-up pirates present the Golden
Crab Claw award to the student who shows
the most promise in four categories.

"The first is eating horrible things."

45

"The second is being loud
in front of old ladies."

"The third is making babies
cry by making a face."

"And the fourth is a good working knowledge of the cabbage."

He shined his fingernails on his chest and looked at them proudly.

"And I won it two years in a row."

The pirate was still waggling his head smugly from side to side when Billy suddenly said, "Does that look like land to the south?"

"What? Where? Land ahoy! LAND AHOY!"

"Twoink!" said the pig.

It was Itchy Ear Island. They reeled in the tree house and climbed on board.

"Mr. Fishcake, you are indeed good at directions," said the pirate once they were ashore. "But what are you good at, Miss Fishnose?"

"Mathematics. Basketball. Essays. Rock climbing. What are you good at, Pirate?" asked Heidi.

"Everything."

"Really? Everything? What about . . . skipping?"

"Good at it. Standing on my hands."

"Disco dancing?"

"Good at it. Pirates disco dance all the time. Didn't you know that?"

"Roller skating?"

"Good at it. The quickest way to get around a ship. Although it is hard on sand."

"Spelling?"

"There's no such thing."

"There is so."

"There can't be. I know everything and I've never heard of this spelling. Therefore, there is no such thing. But if there was, I'd be good at it."

Billy grinned. Heidi was fuming again. She was very good at spelling, and she'd forgotten to include it in her list.

"And how are you at spitting, Miss Fishnose?" asked the pirate.

"What?" said Heidi.

"Spitting. Spitting! Are you good at that, too?"

Heidi nodded slowly. She was good at spitting, although it wasn't something that she usually bragged about.

"Good," said the pirate. He spread the picture of Itchy Ear Island out on the sand. "Because this here treasure map won't *look* like a treasure map until someone grumpy spits on it . . ."

Heidi gaped at him.

" . . . with a parrot sitting on the top of her . . . or his . . . head."

The pirate looked at Billy.

"Any spitter worth his or her salt knows that. Are you sure she is telling the truth about her spitting ability?"

Billy shrugged.

"I'm a stupendous spitter," yelled Heidi. "But that's not a parrot, it's a pig."

"There she goes again, Polly. Jump on her head so that she can spit on the map. Don't bite her on the ear, mind you. She can't help it if she doesn't know what a real parrot looks like."

He looked nervously at the late afternoon sun.

"Well, go on then, Miss Fishnose. The clock's a-tickin', you know."

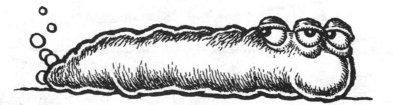

Heidi let the pig climb onto her head and then, with a dubious look at the pirate, she spat on the paper.

Nothing happened for a moment. But then the island in the picture began to turn into red jelly. The jelly slurped and burbled, and slowly spread out toward the edges of the paper.

Tiny jelly hills began to poke up where the picture had been. Next, a river appeared, running between two of the hills. Palm trees as big as matchsticks grew up by the river, which ran onto a little beach.

Finally, when it was a complete map, everything flattened with a loud slurp! and the jelly-paper rolled itself up tight.

Just then, Heidi cried out in delight.
The beach around them was suddenly
teeming with strange, brightly colored
seashells, which were emerging from the
waves in row after row.

"What are they?" asked Heidi.
"They're beautiful."

"Oh, sea horse dribble!"

The pirate slapped himself on the
forehead.

"**Ponder crabs!** This is the time of
day they come ashore. We can't get past
them. They don't like to be disturbed,
and we don't want to make them angry."

"Why? What will they do?" asked Heidi.

"Well, Miss Fishnose, they will nip and tickle our feet until we all fall over. I've seen many a pirate lying helpless on the sand, unable to stop giggling. It's not pretty. So we will just have to wait."

"Twoink," said the pig.

"That's right, Polly. Unless we can think of a question that they don't know the answer to. Then we can sneak across the beach, because they always scuttle back to the edge of the ocean to ponder."

"I know a question," said Billy. "I actually know a lot of questions. Like . . . how many grains of sand are there on the beach?"

The ponder crabs stirred.

"And why don't cats bark?"

The crabs looked at each other, up at the sky, and back to each other. Then they began to dance slowly from side to side. As they danced, their shells rubbed together, making a strange, low humming sound.

"Do sea urchins have parents? Can sea worms see? Can mermaids count past ten?"

The humming grew stronger and higher, louder and louder, as the dancing sped up and the crabs began to leap into the air. Then they scurried over to the water's edge to watch the waves while they pondered Billy's questions.

The pig darted across the beach, leading Billy, Heidi, and the pirate to safety.

"Right, then," said the pirate when they were on safer ground. "We start from that tree over there that looks a bit like a . . . a pelican." He shuddered, then shook his head. They set off for the tree.

"Ten steps to the west, four steps backward, then three more forward, and another two backward."

"That's ten minus four plus three minus two. That equals seven," yelled Heidi. "Take seven steps forward."

"In that direction." Billy pointed.

"I knew that, Miss Fishnose," said the pirate. "You're not telling me anything I don't already know."

Suddenly a peanut flew out from a bush. Then another. And another.

"Well ginger me beer! It's Berry Berry Barry Barton."

The pirate pointed accusingly at the bush.

"I know you're in there, Berry Berry Barry. Still got plenty of peanuts, I see."

A peanut flew past his ear.

"We're looking for treasure. We're not washing, you know. If you want to come out and help us you can. Or are you hiding from the . . ."

He squinted at the sky, then quickly took seven steps west and looked back at the map.

"Five steps to the south, then another four. Then two steps backward, and six forward."

"Five plus four minus two plus six equals thirteen. Take thirteen steps," yelled Heidi.

"That way." Billy pointed again.

"Polly, fly over and get the shovel by my clothesline," said the pirate. "Bring it here in your snout . . . I mean beak."

He looked back to the bush.

"You'd better not have taken it, Berry Berry Barry. I know you like to dig for peanuts."

Another peanut flew out of the bush.

The pirate ignored it and paced out thirteen steps to the south.

"This is the spot. This is the spot."

The pirate stood to attention and saluted.

"And now we dig."

Together, they took turns with the shovel to dig a deep hole.

Then the pirate threw down the shovel, jumped into the hole, and pulled out an old, battered sea chest.

"**Treasure chest! Treasure chest!** Get ready to dive your hands into the treasure and laugh loudly."

He opened the lid, and the gold and silver gleamed in the setting sun. Bright red rubies as big as apples fell through his fingers as he plunged his hands into the chest and began to laugh.

"Ha ha ha! HA HA! HA HA HA!"

He looked at Billy and Heidi.

"Your turn."

They sank their hands into the treasure and began to giggle.

"Tee hee hee. Tee hee. Hee hee."

"Pepper me bones! What do you call that squiddly noise, sailors? Laugh from your butter belly. Especially you, Miss Fishnose. You're far too grumpy."

Heidi and Billy began to laugh.
"Ha Ha Ha! Ha Ha Ha!
HA HA!"

At that moment, the sun hit the horizon.

The pirate yelped.

"Oh, no! It's getting dark! You know what that means—I've got to go. Can't stay. Nice to see you. Come again soon. Bye bye."

"But wait," said Billy. "Do we take the treasure with us?"

"Pirates don't take treasure, Mr. Fishcake. They just search for it."

And with that, he turned and ran.

"See you on washing day, Berry Berry Barry," he yelled over his shoulder.

He was already on the roof of the tree house when Billy and Heidi reached the shore.

"Come on! All aboard! **Paddle, sailors! Paddle!**"

As they paddled out to the house,
strange shadows began to fill the air. . . .

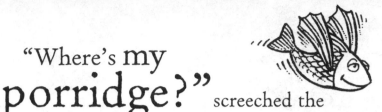

"Where's my **porridge?**" screeched the pirate, as he hurled himself down next to the chimney and huddled there with his bottom high in the air.

Billy and Heidi hoisted the sail and leaned to the right.

"Come on," cried the pirate. "We're in a hurry, you know!"

Finally, the house sailed away from the island.

The pig collapsed against Heidi's leg. Heidi and Billy were smiling as they looked out over the mighty ocean.

The pirate raised his head furtively skyward, but with his eyes shut tight.

"Do you see any pelicans, Miss Fishnose?" he squeaked.

Heidi shook her head.

"What about you, Mr. Fishcake? See any?"

Billy shook his head, too, but kept
watching the sky just in case.

"Right, here's the plan. One of us
will have to climb into bed and pull the
blankets over their head so the giant
pelicans can't find him . . . or her. The other
two will have to sail this fish-stick house
home.

"We have to have a vote. But you are
only children, and children can't vote.
I'm a pirate and I can. So . . . all those who
think that I should climb into bed and pull
the blankets over my head so the giant
pelicans can't find me, raise your hand."

The pirate raised his hand and
pretended to look around.

"Okay, that's it, then. I'll have to do it."

"Where's my porridge?"

And do you know what?
He did.